THE INFINITE FOREST

The Infinite Forest

First Edition : February, 2026

ISBN : 978-93-47125-42-3

Publisher : **Unbound Script**
2/41, Ansari Road,
Daryaganj, Delhi-110002
Website : www.unboundscript.com
E-mail : books@unboundscript.com
Contact No. : 011-35807601

THE INFINITE FOREST
by Rashmi Kaushik & Dr. Surabhee Kaushik Saha

Price : ₹ 499/-

Printer : Yash Printographics, Noida, U.P.

THE INFINITE FOREST

RASHMI KAUSHIK
DR. SURABHEE KAUSHIK SAHA

FOREWORD

The first-time author Rashmi Kaushik spread out her 30-feet long, 50 panels of detailed, diligent, hand drawn art illustrations on a dining table of a restaurant, I was awestruck by the magnitude of the project.

How many days had she spent bending over these canvases sculpting every leaf, branch and tree of the dense forest? Weeks, months, maybe years, more?

Did the altering skyline awaken her dreams, was she troubled by the now glowing, now fading sun and the moon or was it cathartic to be engulfed in an alternate, more artistic reality?

"This is magnetic and it deserves to be converted into a book.", I said to her after a long silence. I continued to stare at the artwork, as strangers joined us mesmerized by what was on display.

It is my privilege to write the foreword for The Infinite Forest which is precious for the juxta-positioning of distinct artforms. This universe was created lovingly by mother Rashmi Kaushik the illustrator and her daughter, Dr. Surabhee Saha the poet. These co-creators combine skills to portray lingering images of a haunting forest inhabited by wandering women.

The book addresses relevant issues, the mysterious magic of forests, the existence of women and compassion for the unseen. These are stories of strength, stories of silence, of desolation, of desire, of nature and of nurturing..
The verses synchronize with the images noiselessly, changing tone as vibrant colours dissolve into pastels and bold strokes settle for tender lines. The Infinite Forest is a journey to self-discovery, poignant and priceless.

- Padma Shri Bhawana Somaaya

Dedicated to
our darling,
Kaushik
the eternal
storyteller.

The Hideout

She loves the view above her
as she walks through the infinite forest;
The sun twinkling softly through the leaves.
She needs to go hide today,
in a special place no one else knows of.
A tree… unlike any other.
What's different about it?
Not much… but it's her tree.
She greets it like an old friend.
She lays her palm flat
on its rosewood colored chest.
She can almost count
all the decades the tree has spent without her.
She wonders if someone like her hid there too.
The tree recognizes her
from the warmth of her skin.
It blushes at how it spent all that time
looking for her,
growing taller and taller,
hopeful it would help her find it.
It giggles that all this while
it kept searching for her in the skies…
only for her to find a home at its roots.
Suddenly, it can hear her snoring softly.
It bends its branches to extend its shadow
and cover her face.
The tree whispers to the forest,
"Let her sleep.
She is safe here….she is safe here."

Forest Map

Follow me

I found a pretty path
on that a pretty someone.
Her walk had intent
her hips swayed,
her shadow danced,
the trees bowed before her.
"Follow me." she said.
"Follow me till you find yourself."
So I did.
I tried to memorize what I saw.
The path softened as I kept going,
like the vision of a forgotten dream.
I followed her for hours I think.
suddenly she disappeared.
I wasn't sure anymore.
Do I keep going?
Do I abandon the path?
I turned around
and saw someone pretty again...
She was walking right behind me...all this time...
Her eyes were starving for something familiar.
"Follow me." I said.
"Follow me till you find yourself."

The Cosmic Pause

She pauses.
Before the morning dew
spills on the leaves,
she steals a minute
to be that which she has always been
and that which she never was.
The Universe peers in
and asks her, “Are you ready? Shall we begin?”
“Give me a minute…” she urges.
“A little bit of the night is still lingering in my eyes.
Come here, come closer and sit next to me…”
The Universe ever loyal,
sits by her side and asks,
“What are we waiting for?”
“I wait for no one.” she laughs.
“But I know-
something has been waiting for me.”

The Offering

River: I don't let anyone near me.
I rejected the Sun even after it brought
me jewels… I devoured the Rocks even
when it promised me protection.
What do you bring?

Her: All I can offer is the thirst of the
Seven Seas.

River: Welcome my beloved, sit down,
dip your feet in my current,
drink till you cannot drink anymore.

The Chosen One

The Wind imitates her.
When she is still,
the air lies motionless,
holding its breath in reverence.

When she is wild,
the Wind grows ravenous,
it's edges sharpened by her mood.
It tangles itself in her hair.
Like a restless lover desperate to touch
what it can never keep.

Together they move as though
the Universe is empty.
As though nothing remains
but the feral Wind
and the Woman it cannot stop chasing.

The world calls it weather.
But the truth is-
the Wind has chosen it's God.

Only I

All that is… is not.
All that shall be… will never be.
All that was… never was.

Only I remain.
Only I endure.
Only I am.

No heavens to rejoice in.
No hell to succumb to.

And when the last light dies,
I will still be here,
watching over the vast nothing.

The Confidant

The Forest is the keeper of all secrets.
The Forest knows
where the deer run and hide.
Only when she is alone,
the deer hop towards her.
She may not know where they hide
but she knows where they can be found.

The Constant

She drapes herself in shades of pink.
The cloth falls on her waist,
exposing the arch.
Her eyes are smudged
with forgotten hymns,
half-shadow and half-dream.
“What’s the occasion?” asked the curious Leaf.
She smiled,
“The world is spinning,
the skies are drifting,
the soil shifts beneath my feet.
The rivers spill over,
the flowers bloom softly and
the colors are so pretty
where the skies and the earth meet.”
The leaf muttered,
“But all of that happened yesterday too.”
She exclaimed, “I know!
Nothing changed!
Isn’t that wondrous?
Is that not worth dressing up for?”

The Walk

If you see her footsteps in the soft soil,
you may think she made them
on her walk to the River.
But that is far from the truth.
The Forest expands and collapses
to accommodate her pretty feet...
And when she reaches the River,
it swallows her sorrows whole.
Like a priest absolving a Goddess.
She, who was worshipped
since before the Rain had a name.
She cups her hands to take quick cool gulps.
The River sighs.... it found a glistening haven,
on the dip of her lip.
Unlike the lotuses
she doesn't wipe off the drops
streaming down her neck.
The River isn't just an old friend.
It knew her when she was born.
It will wait for her like time has waited for sand.
You see the Forest does not control or collect...
It exists in her grandiose.
It will collapse with her exit.

The Morning After

Forest: Where have you been?
Her: Wherever you take me.
Forest: I didn't see you in the morning.
Her: But I spent the night in your arms.
Forest: I missed you.
Her: I never left.

Darling Footsteps

She looks for God everywhere.
Whenever she takes her morning walks.
Every morning,
the twigs, the leaves, the deer,
wait for her darling footsteps.
They stare at her in awe.
“Settle down.” they whisper.
“The little Goddess is taking her walk.”

Unquenchable

Forest: What did you find today?

Her: The rumors of the woods and
stories from the smooth river
pebbles, both fact and fiction.
A few whispers from the foxes.
Some mist from the leaves.
A few haikus the rain left behind.
And some cool water…
for my unquenchable thirst.

Iktara

The birds wait for her.
She is the maker of all melodies.
They sing to stir her
with their wings full of joy,
until the hour comes for them
to find their way home.

Which is strange…
for she is both the first step of every journey
and the only door they return to.

Rhythm and Ruin

She is the favorite of the peacocks.
They knew her before
they knew how to dance.
They know her eyes, her bright body and
the softness of her siren song.
They stole colors from the cosmos and
wrapped themselves in the blues of midnight
just for her.
She is their Goddess and Monster.
Both Rhythm and Ruin.

Golden

The Sun grew soft in her shadows.
He slipped between the ribs
of the never-ending trees,
like a golden trespasser,
just to catch a glimpse of her.

She lay against the spine of an old tree,
fingers playing with a single blade of grass.

The Sun is all-powerful, all-knowing,
lover of every living thing.
The eternal rival to Rain and Thunder.

Yet he longs to be the blade of grass,
she holds between her lips,
the bright green trembling against her breath.

She stretches her arms.
He leans in closer.
Her cool palms nearly reach the shimmering sky.
He smiles to himself.
"This is enough, even this much is enough
to rise again tomorrow."

Orange Moon

She has always loved the Moon.
Perhaps even before they conspired to
invent the foam of the sea.
It was her idea to add the salt.

Sometimes,
the Moon strips itself bare,
shedding every borrowed hue.

“Too improper?” the Moon whispers.
“Not at all!” she laughs.
Her laughter curling through the dark.
“I always feel as though I haven’t seen enough of you.”

She is a constant;
while the Moon is a shapeshifter.
And yet,
neither truly changes,
and neither ever stays the same.

Unravelling

The cloth she draped over herself
slipped from her shoulder…
Did someone see her?

If yes- what did they see?
That her shoulders and neck
were carved from eternal ruin,
or that her navel holds
the secrets of existence itself?
Perhaps no one saw her…
and if so- how tragic.
Gather the stars,
summon the Moon and the Sun.
The night was not made just for dreaming.

Flight

The branches grow watching her hair…
tangling and untangling,
floating in the wind.
Even the birds watch her before
they leap from their nests.

Forest Hues

No one really believes her,
when she talks of the colors she has seen.
The Infinite Forest is home to every hue,
both odd and familiar.
The pigments weave stories untold,
throughout the known and unknown universe.
The best one… by far
is the color on her face
made by the shade of the Forest.
The greys of the shadows
and the lovely warmth of her skin…
give birth to a new color.
A color that cannot exist beyond the trees.
A color she made with the Forest.
A color the Forest made just for her.

The Return

"Tell the Storms,
their daughter has returned home."

The Infinite Forest

One day I asked, “When did it begin?”
She giggled, “It never began.”
I sighed, “When shall it end?”
She sang, “It cannot end.”

I smiled, “And all that happens in between?”
She echoed, “That’s the trick.
It is, if you are.”
I wasn’t convinced, “If I am?”
She insisted, “It can’t be a question darling.”
Puzzled, I said, “I am…”
She whispered, “I don’t understand doubt.”
“I am!”, I roared.
She blinked in awe, “Oh there you are!
I have been looking for you everywhere.”

The Deleted Epilogue

I: Who made me? What will destroy me?

Her: Creation and Destruction are divine pranksters... neither truly exists, each pretends to be the other.

I: How? Destruction only destroys...Creation only builds.

Her: Not always. Sometimes Destruction renews all that is forgotten and Creation ends all that exists.

I: Impossible!

Her: For instance flowers are formidable destroyers.

I: No, they are gentle creators, artists even...

Her: Well, Destruction is art. Flowers teach us gentle destruction. A flower shatters the seed it grows from and splits the soil that gives it a home.
On the other hand, fire is a violent creator. Fire has created a lot more than it has ever destroyed. It is divinely entangled with the Sun, the first of the Gods and the last of the creators.

Artist's Note:

How was the book conceived? The conception to completion is an exciting journey of ideas. I wanted to create an artist book full of illustrations and poetry. I envisioned that the visual landscape, would carry with it verses which would fulfill both art lovers and poetry readers. This book is a map of beautiful destinations through imagery.
As an artist, I often have been asked why women dominate my illustrations. My answer is, "Why not?".
The book is for all those who celebrate longing and anyone who wishes to master the power of knowing. This book gently calls out to you to return long after you've put the book down. These are all stories in verse celebrating womanhood and the universe she births and nurtures. I am grateful to you my dear reader, this book has found a home in your hands!
I thank all those who supported me in this journey, my publishers for the firm trust in this artscape and to my daughter for bringing verses to my hand drawn universe.

Much Warmth,
- Rashmi Kaushik

Poet's Note:

Every word I wrote, I wrote because the art invoked in me all that is familiar and unknown. The words exist because of the ethereal imagery of the artist, giving me the opportunity to be a priestess offering prayer in the scared temple of The Infinite Forest. I hope it brings you, my beloved reader, the comfort you have been looking for, and the limitless love you never knew existed. The Infinite Forest is best enjoyed under a blanket, on a cozy afternoon. Every character, every detail and nuance reminded me of my path. I took the scenic route and every poem brought me back to myself. I hope the readers find the same solace in reading and exploring The Infinite Forest as much as we enjoyed creating this. The book was made in reverse, meaning the art came first and then the images inspired the poetry. This universe is custom made for those who don't really care for the rules.

It's so nice to finally meet you,
- Dr. Surabhee Kaushik Saha

About the Artist-

Rashmi Kaushik is a veteran journalist and wrote for The Times of India & Press Trust of India. She is also a collaborative author & mentor of Ink & Stardust: Stories in Verse (Scholastic), a landmark book 'by the children, for the children'. Rashmi is an educator, an artist and a storyteller.
She cares deeply about art and its impact on the world. Rashmi believes that the entire universe is bound by art and stories.

Insta Id: @rashmikoushik2000

About the Poet-

Dr. Surabhee Kaushik Saha specializes in data analytics and is a passionate illustrator. Surabhee is a storyteller who creates at the crossroads of emotion, imagination, and art. Her work flows between words, images, and feeling—transforming inner worlds into living landscapes. Through The Infinite Forest, she invites readers into a realm where creativity becomes refuge, memory becomes color, and poetry becomes a form of quiet magic.
She is the daughter of Rashmi and a lover of kitsch art, movies, poetry and biryani.

Insta Id: @surabhee13

Rashmi (2025) at Manhattan Beach, California. The book was first created as a handmade concertina.
A lovely waitress watched Rashmi unfold her raw handmade artwork and measured the long scroll of art- it spanned over 30 feet!